Mighty Min

Melissa Castrillón

ALISON
GREEN
BOOKS

Min lives with her four small-but-mighty aunts,
Flora, Lily, Olive and Clementine, in a tiny house
at the bottom of a garden. Every night they gather
round the fire, and the aunts tell stories of their
extraordinary deeds.

Here's mighty Aunt Olive, telling how she once
saved Min from a hawk.

Every night,
Min listens wide-eyed
as each aunt tells her tale.

And then it's bedtime.

But one night,
Min couldn't sleep.

She kept thinking about her aunts' amazing stories.

"I'll never have a story of my own," she thought, sadly. "I'm too small and not nearly mighty enough."

So it was quite a shock when a strange voice said . . .

"Aha! You're just the right size!"

Then a pair of huge claws picked Min up . . .

and whisked her away through the night.

"Don't bother eating me!" shouted Min. "I'm not much of a meal."

"Eat you?" hooted a voice. "That would hardly be wise."

The owl
(because that's what it was)
plopped Min on the ground
with a bump.

"There's a monster in the garden," it said, "and it's causing all kinds of chaos. The animals are in trouble. Will you help them?"

Min gulped. "I'm not very mighty," she said. "But I'll do my best. Who's first?"

"Me!"
cried a rabbit.
"The monster frightened
my babies away, and now I
can't find them anywhere."
"No problem!"
said Min.

She was good at hide-and-seek,

and she soon found all those long-eared babies.

"Right," said Min, "who's next?"

"Me!" called a mouse.
"The monster chased me through some
brambles and my tail got knotted up."
"No problem!" said Min.

Her aunts had taught her all
about knots, and her small hands
made quick work of them.

"Right," said Min, "who's next?"
Lots of little voices called out . . .

. . . and Min was kept busy all night.

She heaved over a beetle that the monster had knocked on its back.

She bandaged a grasshopper's leg that the monster had bashed with its paw.

She coaxed two terrified snails out of their shells.

Min was starting to feel quite cross with this monster.
"I bet my aunts would know how to tame it," she said.
"Oh, no!" said the animals. "No one can tame the monster.
It's got long sharp claws! And big fierce eyes!
And huge pointy ears! And . . .

"...it's coming right now!

Run, Min! Hide!
The monster will get you!"

Min was very scared, but she
thought of her mighty little aunts.
"No! I won't hide!" she said. "I'm going
to tell that monster off for
everything it's done."

But then she turned around.

A cat really is a monster,
when you're as small
as little Min.

She ducked
and dived,

clambered
and swung
as the cat
chased after her.

"Stop that!"
she shouted.
"I'm not a mouse!"
Then she had an idea.

She scrambled up the tallest
stem she could find, leapt
on the cat's back and, with
her little hands, she went . . .

tickly, tickly, TICKLE!

The cat started purring like an engine.
"Hah!" laughed Min. "You're just a big softie, aren't you!"
The other animals peeped out in astonishment.
Min had tamed the monster!

The sun was coming up,
and it was time to go home.
"Come on, everyone!" cried Min.
"Let's go back for breakfast!"
With a hoot, two squeaks and
a purr, they set off together.

When the aunts woke up that morning,
Min's bed was empty.

"Where is she?" they said.
"It's not like Min to miss breakfast."
They were very worried – especially when they heard
the noisy rumble of a cat purring. They ran outside.

"Help!" they cried.
"The cat's got her!"

"Oh, no it hasn't!
Min's got the cat!
Clever Min! Brave Min!
Mighty Min!"

Mighty Min
and her friends ate
a mighty breakfast.

And that night Min had
her own mighty tale to tell!

First published in the UK in 2019 by Alison Green Books
An imprint of Scholastic Children's Books
Euston House, 24 Eversholt Street London NW1 1DB
A division of Scholastic Ltd
www.scholastic.co.uk
London – New York – Toronto – Sydney – Auckland
Mexico City – New Delhi – Hong Kong
Designed by Zoë Tucker

HB ISBN: 978 1 407185 30 9
PB ISBN: 978 1 407185 31 6

For Luke – my best friend
husband, mighty feminist
and constant champion
of kindness